Rabbit & Squirrel

A Tale of War & Peas

Kara LaReau   Scott Magoon

HARCOURT, INC. Orlando Austin New York San Dieg

Text copyright © 2008 by Kara LaReau
Illustrations copyright © 2008 by Scott Magoon

www.HarcourtBooks.com

Library of Congress Cataloging-in-Publication Data
LaReau, Kara.
Rabbit and Squirrel/Kara LaReau; Scott Magoon.
p. cm.
Summary: Rabbit and Squirrel are neighbors who never even say hello
until someone starts damaging their gardens, and then they blame one
another and start a fight that continues even after they meet the real culprit.
[1. Neighborliness—Fiction. 2. Fighting (Psychology)—Fiction.
3. Gardening—Fiction. 4. Rabbits—Fiction. 5. Squirrels—Fiction.]
I. Magoon, Scott, ill. II. Title.
PZ7.L32078Rab 2008
[E]—dc22   2006101618
ISBN 978-0-15-206307-8

C E G H F D B

Printed in Singapore

The illustrations in this book were created digitally.
The display type was created by Scott Magoon.
The text type was set in Chaloops.
Color separations by Colourscan Co. Pte. Ltd., Singapore
Printed and bound by Tien Wah Press, Singapore
Production supervision by Christine Witnik
Designed by April Ward

TOMATOES

For those who would prefer
more peas and less war
—K. L.

For Grampy, who *always*
shared his garden
—S. M.

Not too long ago,
there lived a rabbit
named Rabbit.

Rabbit was very proud of her garden.
She tended her carrots and lettuce
with tremendous effort and care.

Across the way,
there lived a squirrel
named Squirrel.

Just as Rabbit was proud of her garden,
Squirrel was proud of his.
He tended his sweet peas and tomatoes
with great energy and zeal.

Though Rabbit and Squirrel
lived right across the way from each other,
they kept to themselves
and never offered each other vegetables
or even bothered to say hello . . .

... until one day
when Rabbit woke up to find
that something awful had happened.

Someone had pulled up
her crunchiest carrots.
Someone had removed
her leafiest lettuce.

Rabbit had a very good idea
who that very bad someone might be.

She hopped over to Squirrel's house
and thumped on his door.

"Hello?" Squirrel said.

"You are a pest!" shouted Rabbit.

"Stay away from my garden—or else!"

The next day,
Squirrel woke up to find
that something awful had happened.

Someone had snapped off
his sweetest sweet peas.
Someone had plucked
his ripest, juiciest tomatoes.

Squirrel had a very good idea
who that very bad someone might be.
He scurried over to Rabbit's house
and scratched on her door.

"What is it?" asked Rabbit.

"You are a pest!" shouted Squirrel.

"Stay away from my garden—or else!"

Then he threw his rottenest tomato at Rabbit's house and scurried away.

The next day,
Squirrel woke up to find
all of his beautiful tomatoes plucked away,
and **all** of his sweet peas snapped off.

"This means **war!**" he shouted,
shaking his fist in Rabbit's direction.

Later, Rabbit was enjoying a nice, big salad. So tasty, she thought. I should have tried tomatoes and peas sooner!

Just then, she heard a horrible rushing sound.

It was the sound of water.

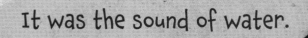

"You've ruined my garden,
and my house!" cried Rabbit,
giving Squirrel a push.
"You are my sworn enemy!"

"Well, you've ruined **my** garden,
so you deserved it," said Squirrel,
giving Rabbit a push.
"You are **my** sworn enemy!"

Just as they were thinking
of worse things to do
to each other . . .

. . . they heard a terrible booming voice from above.

"WHAT HAPPENED TO MY GARDEN?"

said the Gardener.

"Your garden?" said Rabbit and Squirrel.

"**GET OUT OF HERE, YOU PESTS!**"

the Gardener shouted.
She waved her pitchfork
and stomped the ground with
her big green boots.

Rabbit and Squirrel
hopped and scurried away
as fast as they could . . .

. . . into the dark woods.

"Nasty squirrel," said Rabbit.
"You've ruined **everything!**"
"Mean old rabbit," said Squirrel.
"**You've** ruined everything!"

And so it went.

Rabbit and Squirrel stayed in the woods
and continued to blame each other.

One of these days, they'll grow tired of fighting.

And then, hopefully, they'll learn to grow
something new.